Rabbids Invasion

Case File #3:
The Accidental Accomplice

by David Lewman
illustrated by Daniel Mather

Simon Spotlight
New York London Toronto Sydney New Delhi

Based on the TV series Rabbids™ Invasion as seen on Nickelodeon™

SIMON SPOTLIGHT
An imprint of Simon & Schuster Children's Publishing Division
1230 Avenue of the Americas, New York, New York 10020
First Simon Spotlight hardcover edition September 2014
© 2014 Ubisoft Entertainment. All rights reserved. Rabbids, Ubisoft, and the Ubisoft logo are trademarks of Ubisoft Entertainment in the U.S. and/or other countries.
Also available in a Simon Spotlight paperback edition.
All rights reserved, including the right of reproduction in whole or in part in any form.
SIMON SPOTLIGHT and colophon are registered trademarks of Simon & Schuster, Inc.
For information about special discounts for bulk purchases, please contact Simon & Schuster Special Sales at 1-866-506-1949 or business@simonandschuster.com.
Manufactured in the United States of America 0814 FFG
10 9 8 7 6 5 4 3 2 1
ISBN 978-1-4814-1720-4 (pbk)
ISBN 978-1-4814-1721-1 (hc)
ISBN 978-1-4814-1722-8 (eBook)

CHAPTER 1:

SMOOSHY LANDING

Early one morning, a huge tanker truck full of butterscotch pudding sped down an empty road just outside a city. The driver, Gus, was in a hurry.

"Can't be late," Gus muttered to himself. "Gotta deliver this pudding while it's still fresh!"

Suddenly . . . *FWOOM!* A blinding white light filled the sky in front of the tanker truck!

"YAAAH!!!" Gus screamed. He couldn't see, which is what usually happens when a light is blinding.

If Gus had been driving down a perfectly straight road, he might have continued along safely until he'd regained his sight.

But it wasn't a perfectly straight road.

In fact, the truck was zooming down a perfectly curved road. And because he was blinded, Gus didn't see that curve. He drove right off the road and slammed into . . . a huge oak tree! CRASH!!! The tank fell over. A valve on the back of the tank broke open. And thousands of gallons of butterscotch pudding spilled onto the ground.

The driver wasn't hurt, but he was knocked out, so he didn't see where the blinding light had come from: a spaceship!

The spaceship looked very unusual. (Not that there are very many usual-looking spaceships.) It was yellow and blue and resembled a submarine, except that it had a face on the front. In the face's black mouth were two big white teeth.

The kind of teeth you see in . . . RABBIDS!

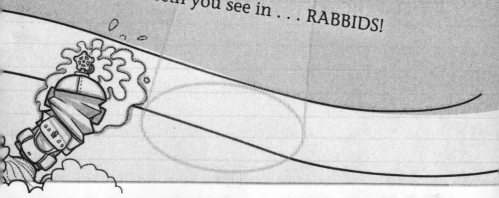

Which made sense, because the spaceship belonged to the Rabbids, those mysterious invaders from . . . who knows where!

SPLOOSH! The spaceship landed right in the middle of the butterscotch pudding. A door opened and three Rabbids ran out. Right into the pudding.

"Bwah?" said the Rabbid in front, looking down at the light-brown pudding covering his feet. The spaceship flew out of sight, but the Rabbids didn't even wave good-bye because they were so interested in the pudding.

"Bwah!" said one of the Rabbids, delighted. He scooped up a handful of pudding and plopped it onto his head. Then he shaped the pudding into several lovely hairstyles.

Another Rabbid saw what the first Rabbid had done. He scooped up some pudding and sculpted it into a thick mustache and a long beard.

The third Rabbid scooped up some pudding too. But what could he shape it into? A vest? A jacket? Then he had a brilliant idea!

PLAP!!! A handful of butterscotch pudding hit the first Rabbid right in the back of the head. He wheeled around and saw the third Rabbid laughing. "BWAH HA HA HA HA!"

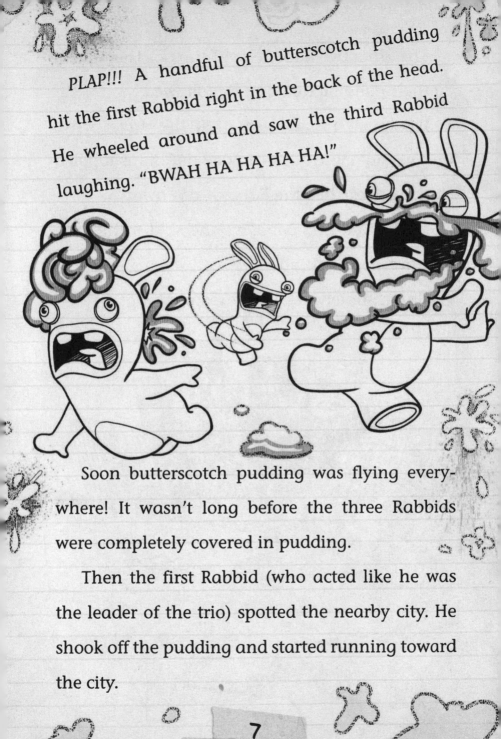

Soon butterscotch pudding was flying everywhere! It wasn't long before the three Rabbids were completely covered in pudding.

Then the first Rabbid (who acted like he was the leader of the trio) spotted the nearby city. He shook off the pudding and started running toward the city.

The other two Rabbids saw him go. They shook off their pudding and quickly followed.

It was at this moment that the driver woke up. Feeling dazed, Gus climbed out of his toppled truck and watched the Rabbids run away.

"Are those . . . Rabbids?" he said to himself. "Or am I seeing things?"

Unfortunately, he wasn't seeing things.

CHAPTER 2:
SECRET AGENT SECOND CLASS

At the Secret Government Agency for the Investigation of Intruders-Rabbid Division (also known as the SGAII-RD), Agent Glyker stood in the hall outside his crummy little office.

His office was small and dingy, and the hallway was unappealing, with ugly brown paint on the walls and dust on the floor. But Agent Glyker didn't mind. He was happily watching the janitor paint a new title on his door:

GLYKER, SECRET AGENT SECOND CLASS

"Yup," Glyker said proudly. "That's me! I used to be Secret Agent Third Class, but I got promoted!"

"Congratulations," the janitor said flatly, not looking up from his work.

"Thank you!" Glyker said enthusiastically. "You're probably wondering what I did to get promoted so quickly."

"Nope," said the janitor, dipping his thin paintbrush into a can of black paint. "Don't really care."

Glyker either didn't hear the janitor's answer or decided to ignore it. "It was nothing, really," he said, pretending to be modest. "Director Stern and I were chasing some Rabbids, and I basically saved his life."

The janitor continued painting letters on the door. He didn't say anything.

Agent Glyker stood there awkwardly for a moment and then said, "I should probably go check in with Director Stern right now. See what my next big assignment is."

The janitor finally looked up at Glyker. "Did you catch one of those troublemaking Rabbids?"

Glyker frowned. "Um, no."

"Then that's probably your next assignment," the janitor said, chuckling.

Agent Glyker strode confidently down the hallway, and knocked on Director Stern's door. "Uncle Jim?" he asked, opening the door.

"DON'T CALL ME THAT!" Director Stern roared. "When you and I are here at work, we are not uncle and nephew. We are Director and . . ." He paused, trying to remember Glyker's title.

"Secret Agent Second Class!" Glyker said helpfully. "Speaking of which, I was wondering what privileges come with my promotion."

"Privileges?" Stern asked, wrinkling his nose as if he were smelling some rotten fruit.

"Right, like, for example," Glyker asked eagerly, "will I be issued my own secret car with lots of super high-tech features?"

"No," Stern answered, shaking his head.

"My own secret parking place?"

"No."

"My own key to the secret nicer bathroom?"

"No way," Stern said firmly. "Out of the question. There is no secret nicer bathroom. And if there were one, it would be for me and me alone. Now go catch me a Rabbid!"

Discouraged by these answers, Agent Glyker turned and started to go back to his office to see how the new title on his door was coming along. Then he thought of something. "Could I at least have full access to the Closet of Super-Secret Spy

Gadgets without having to ask for special permission? Otherwise, it's like my promotion means nothing!"

Director Stern hesitated. The truth was, Agent Glyker's promotion did mean nothing. It was a made-up title. And Stern didn't really want to give his nephew full access to the Closet of Super-Secret Spy Gadgets. On the other hand, if he didn't,

his sister might be mad at him for mistreating her son. And his sister could be really mean.

"Fine," he said. "You can have full access. Now if you wouldn't mind, I'd like to have full access to my office . . . WITHOUT YOU IN IT!"

"Thanks, Uncle Jim!" Glyker said, forgetting he wasn't supposed to call his uncle that at work. Before Stern could bellow

"DON'T CALL ME THAT!" Glyker was hurrying down the hallway to the Closet of Super-Secret Spy Gadgets.

There was one item in particular he'd had his eye on for a long time. . . .

CHAPTER 3:

A MYSTERIOUS PLACE

At the same time that Agent Glyker was talking to Director Stern, the three Rabbids were standing in a line of people outside a big place. They had no idea what they were waiting in line for. They just saw people lining up, and they joined them.

19

In front of them, they saw people handing little pieces of cardboard to a man. The man scanned the pieces of cardboard, handed them back to the people, and let them pass through the turnstile.

When the Rabbids reached the front of the line, the man held out his hand for their tickets.

But they didn't have tickets.

"Bwah bwah-bwah bwah bwah bwah," the leader said, as though that explained everything. He started to walk under the turnstile, but the man stopped him.

"Whoa, whoa! Hold it right there!" he said. "You gotta have a ticket to get into the stadium."

The Rabbids looked puzzled. They had no idea what the man was saying.

The third Rabbid got an idea. He found a candy wrapper on the ground, picked it up, and handed it to the man.

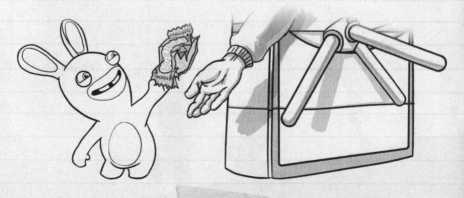

"That's not a ticket!" the man snarled angrily.

"Now, go on! Get out of here!"

The Rabbids just stood there staring at him.

Then the man pulled his foot back and kicked the nearest Rabbid in the butt. "BWAH!" the Rabbid yelled. The Rabbids got out of line and walked away. But they didn't go far.

When they were out of the man's sight, they hurried over to the wall of the big building. There must be some way to get in! (Without getting kicked in the butt.) This place looked really interesting. And it smelled interesting too.

They hadn't gone very far around the wall when they saw a man unloading boxes of hot dogs from a truck. He put the boxes on a golf cart until it couldn't hold any more. Then the driver of the golf cart drove off . . . right into the stadium!

The three Rabbids looked at each other. "Bww-waaah . . . ," they said, grinning. They knew just what to do.

The truck driver finished filling the back of another golf cart with boxes of hot dogs. As the golf cart sped off, the driver turned back to his truck to get more boxes. If he had watched the golf cart go, he would have seen something surprising: three Rabbids sitting on the golf cart's back bumper, waving!

Once the golf cart was inside the stadium, the Rabbids jumped off. They stood and looked around.

A bunch of big guys walked by wearing baseball hats and carrying snacks. One of them
pumped his fist in the air and they all whooped.
"WHOOO!"

The three Rabbids walked behind them, trying
to swagger like the big guys. They pumped their
fists in the air and yelled, "Bwhoo bwhoo!" The
guys turned around, but didn't see anyone because
the Rabbids were so much shorter than they were.

They shrugged and went off to find their seats.

One of the Rabbids spotted a vendor selling
peanuts. "Peanuts! Get your peanuts!" he called.

The Rabbid picked a couple of empty boxes out of a trash can and held them up. "Bwah bwah!" he called. "Bwah bwah bwah bwah!"

The three Rabbids had been walking up long ramps and down concrete hallways. Suddenly, they saw a staircase leading down to a beautiful, green field.

"Bwooooooh," the Rabbids crooned, impressed. The leader started running down the stairs toward the field.

And the other two Rabbids ran right behind him. . . .

CHAPTER 4:
YOU'RE OUT!

The manager of the base-ball stadium was yelling so loud, Agent Glyker had to hold his phone away from his ear. "RABBIDS ARE RUINING THE GAME! THEY'RE OUT OF CONTROL! THIS IS A DISASTER!!!"

Glyker drove to the stadium as fast as he could. Waving his identification badge, he sprinted inside.

What he found wasn't pretty.

All the fans were standing up, cupping their hands around their mouths, and booing. "BOOOO! BOOOO!"

The players were standing in the dugouts, wondering what to do.

And three Rabbids were running around the field, messing with everything they could get their hands on. They rolled their feet on bats like they were logs. They dove on the bases and slid in the dirt. They buried the balls in the pitcher's mound as if they were giant round seeds.

The whole time, they kept laughing. "BWAH HA HA HA HA HA!"

Security guards and umpires chased the Rabbids, but they were too hard to catch. They rolled balls and bats at their pursuers to trip them. Sometimes they disappeared into hiding places, only to pop up the second the umpires tried to start the game again.

"BOOOO!!!" roared the crowd. They started throwing trash onto the field, trying to hit the Rabbids. The little invaders thought this was wonderful. They collected the trash and wore some of it as clothing, popped some into their mouths, and threw the rest back into the stands.

"I've got to act fast," Glyker thought, "before this

turns into a full-scale riot! Luckily, I brought along a little surprise for the Rabbids."

He reached into his coat pocket and pulled out the super-secret gadget he'd had his eye on for quite a while. He cradled the small gizmo in his hand and put his finger on the trigger.

It was the Stopomizer.

All he had to do was aim the Stopomizer at

one of the Rabbids, pull the trigger, and . . . *BRZZZT!* The Rabbid would be stopped in his troublemaking tracks. Then Agent Glyker would simply stroll over and pick up the Rabbid. It'd be like carrying a statue. (Not too heavy a statue, he hoped. His back was still a little sore from his last run-in with a Rabbid.) After a short while, the Rabbid would become unstopped and feel just fine.

He snuck down the stairs toward the field, hoping to get as close as possible to the green grass without the Rabbids noticing him. He wasn't sure if these were the same Rabbids he'd met before, but he didn't want to take a chance of being recognized. Glyker assumed the Rabbids thought  of him as their greatest enemy. Perhaps they told each other tales of their encounters with their great and resourceful nemesis.

He managed to find an out-of-the-way corner

behind a low wall. Peeking over it, he spotted a Rabbid not too far away.

The Rabbid had found a catcher's mask and was trying to figure out what to do with it. At the moment, the Rabbid was scooping up dirt near home plate and sifting it with the mask.

Glyker was pretty sure the Rabbid was within range of the Stopomizer. He raised the gadget and carefully aimed it at the Rabbid. Then he took a deep breath, held it, and . . .

"STOP! DON'T SHOOT!"

CHAPTER 5:
COURTNEY

A teenager with short red hair stood right in front of Agent Glyker with her hands stretched out. "DON'T SHOOT!" she repeated.

"Shhh!" Glyker hissed. He didn't want the crowd in the stands to hear someone shouting about shooting. They might panic and stampede. He also didn't want the Rabbids to escape. "Where did you come from?" he asked. "Who are you?"

The girl glared at the agent suspiciously. "I might ask you the same thing!" she said.

Glyker held up his identification badge. "I'm Agent Glyker with the SGAII-RD."

The girl looked puzzled. "I have no idea what that is," she said.

"It's the Secret Government Agency for the Investigation of Intruders-Rabbid Division," he explained.

She rolled her eyes. "Rabbids don't need to be investigated!" she said forcefully. "They need to be protected. I *adore* Rabbids! They are *so* cute! The second I read on Twitter that there were Rabbids at the baseball game today, I hurried down here

as fast as I could. I just love them! I love their eyes, and their ears, and their fur, and—"

Agent Glyker sighed. "Look, uh . . . what did you say your name was?"

"I didn't say," the girl said. "If you were a good secret agent, you'd remember that."

"Fine," Glyker said, clenching his teeth. (He didn't like being told he wasn't good at his job.) "What is your name, then?"

"Courtney," she said. "What's yours?"

"Glyker."

"Thank you very much!" she exclaimed triumphantly. "Glyker! Now I can tell the security guys who was going to shoot the cuddly, adorable little Rabbids! They will probably have you arrested."

Speaking of the Rabbids, what were they doing? Agent Glyker quickly glanced past Courtney to check the baseball field. The Rabbids were still out there, running around and picking up equipment, much to the annoyance of the fans.

"There's no need to call for security," Glyker said quickly. "I am security. And I wasn't going to hurt the Rabbids." He held up the Stopomizer. "This isn't a gun. It's a Stopomizer. It temporarily stops its targets from moving. Not forever. Just for a little while. And it doesn't hurt them."

Courtney nodded as though she was considering what he was saying. Glyker started to relax.
Then she screamed, "SECURITY!!!"

Almost instantly, two big guys in navy jackets and baseball caps appeared. "What's goin' on here?" the bigger one growled in a deep, gruff voice.

Glyker held up his badge. "I'm Agent Glyker, Secret Agent Second Class. I'm here to capture a Rabbid."

The other security guard laughed hollowly. "Ha! A Rabbid? Why don't you hurry up and capture ALL of them? They're ruining the game!"

That was all the permission Glyker needed.
With a triumphant smirk at Courtney, he aimed
his Stopomizer at the nearest Rabbid . . . but
Courtney ran out onto the baseball field scream-
ing, "RUN! RUN, RABBIDS! RUN FOR YOUR CUTE
LITTLE LIVES!"

All three Rabbids stopped what they were doing and looked at Courtney. They pointed at the screaming redhead and laughed. "BWAH HA HA HA!"

"THIS WAY!" shouted Courtney. Waving her hand frantically, she ran into the players' tunnel that led off the field. Imitating her waves and screams, the Rabbids followed her, thinking Courtney was the funniest thing they'd ever seen.

Glyker tried to run out onto the baseball field to chase the Rabbids, but the two big security guards stopped him.

"Hold it right there, pal," the bigger one said. "Now that those pesky Rabbids are off the field, no one goes out there but the players."

Sure enough, the players were trotting back onto the baseball field. Within moments, the game had resumed. Much to Glyker's annoyance, the big video screen showed a picture of Courtney. Underneath were the words, "OUR HERO."

By the time Glyker made his way around the stadium and down to the players' exit, the Rabbids were long gone.

CHAPTER 6

RIDE, RABBIDS, RIDE!

The three Rabbids followed the strange redheaded creature out of the big place with the green field, laughing and mimicking her. "BWAH HA HA HA!"

But when they got a couple of blocks away from the baseball stadium, Courtney turned around and faced them. She stood with her fists on her hips, looking determined.

"Bwhuh?" said the Rabbid who seemed to be the leader. What did this weird Earth person want?

"There," Courtney said. "I saved you! You should be safe as long as you stay away from that awful man, Glyker! Do you think you can do that?"

The Rabbids stared at her. They had no idea what she was saying. They talked among themselves, trying to figure out what was going on.

The Rabbids agreed that Courtney was funny, but crazy, so they should probably get away from her. As they said this, they nodded.

Courtney thought their nodding meant they agreed with her. "Good!" she said. "Just be careful! I've got to go home, but I'll see you soon . . . I hope!"

She ran off. The Rabbids watched her go. Then they looked around. Now what?

Suddenly one of them pointed. "BWAH!" he shouted.

The other two looked to see what he was pointing at. "Bwhooo . . . ," they gasped.

Shining in the afternoon sun was a long row of grocery shopping carts. They were parked in the cart area of a grocery store across the street.

The Rabbids liked how the sun made the metal carts sparkle. They watched as a shopper rolled his empty cart into the long row and left it there. He got in his car and drove off.

The leader gestured for the other two Rabbids to follow him. He ran across the street to the shopping carts. He didn't know what he wanted the cart for, but he knew he wanted it.

The three Rabbids grabbed the cart at the end and tugged on it with all their might. "BWUH! BWUH! BWUH!"

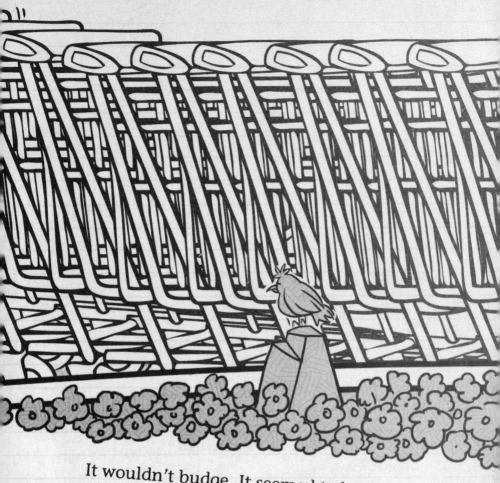

It wouldn't budge. It seemed to be stuck.

The three Rabbids plopped down on the parking lot, discouraged. But then one of them spotted a shopper approaching with an empty cart. They could hear one of the wheels squeaking. *Squeak! Squeak! Squeak!*

Before the shopper could shove the cart in with the others, the Rabbids jumped in front of her cart holding up their hands. "BWAH!" the leader yelled.

"YAAAH!!!" screamed the shopper, startled by the three invaders. She left her cart, ran to her car, jumped in, and peeled out of the parking lot.

"Bwaaah," said the leader, satisfied. He couldn't reach all the way up to the cart's handle, so he grabbed a bar near the bottom of the shopping cart and pushed. He started running around the parking lot, pushing the cart in front of him. "BWHEEEE!"

The other two Rabbids watched their leader, jealous that he had one of the shiny things and they didn't. Then one of them got an idea. He ran up to the cart, jumped up, grabbed the top edge, and hauled himself up into the cart. Now he was riding, and the leader hadn't even noticed!

"Bwah!" said the third Rabbid. What a great idea! He, too, dashed across the parking lot and leaped up into the cart. The two Rabbids in the cart giggled quietly, not wanting to let the leader know they were getting a free ride.

"Bwhoo," sighed the leader. It seemed to him that the cart was getting harder and harder to push. He'd been running with his arms stretched out in front of him, pushing the cart, looking straight down at the ground.

Now he looked up. And saw the other two Rabbids riding in the cart.

"BWAH!" he bellowed. "BWAH BWAH BWAH BWAH BWAH!"

He seemed to be ordering them to get out of the cart. They did, slowly and reluctantly. Then the leader clambered up into the cart and pointed at the other two. "BWAH BWAH BWAH!" he shouted.

He wanted a ride.

Soon the other two Rabbids were pushing the leader around the parking lot as fast as they could go. "BWHEEEEE!" the leader said, delighted.

But it didn't take very long before the two Rabbids grew tired of pushing the leader. All of them loved to ride, but none of them liked to push.

They tried giving the cart a push and then jumping up onto it, so all three could ride, but they didn't go very far.

They were all sitting in the cart, arguing about who should push, when the leader spotted something nearby.

It was a street. But not a flat, boring street. It was a street that sloped sharply downhill. And the hill kept going down for several blocks.

"Bwah!" the leader exclaimed, delighted.

He explained his idea to the other two Rabbids.

They thought it was an *excellent* idea.

CHAPTER 7:

HEY, THAT LOOKS FUN!

"BWHEEEE!!!" the Rabbids screamed as they zoomed down the long hill in the shopping cart.

Cars, bicyclists, and pedestrians had to veer and leap to get out of their way.

HONK! "HEY! WATCH WHERE YOU'RE GOING!"

At the bottom of the big hill, they reached the edge of a city park. The cart jumped the curb and kept right on going straight into the park.

CRASH!!! The shopping cart slammed into a huge sycamore tree, sending the three Rabbids flying. They tumbled through

the grass and came to a stop, groaning.

But the leader stopped groaning almost immediately, because he'd seen something amazing. A young guy with some kind of hard shell on his head had been sliding along, and then he'd just disappeared!

The Rabbids crept forward to investigate.

They heard a strange sound, kind of like a low growl, only smoother.

Finally, they saw what had happened to the young guy with the hard shell on his head. He rolled up out of a hole in the ground on a board with wheels. Then he rolled back down into the hole again.

62

The Rabbids had found a skateboarding park. The sound they'd heard was the sound of skateboard wheels on concrete.

"Bwaaaah . . . ," they said, amazed by the wondrous sight.

The three creatures crawled around a hedge near the skateboarding bowl, which looked like a deep, curved swimming pool without any water in it. They watched as skateboarders dropped down into the bowl on their boards, zoomed across the concrete, rode up the side of the bowl, and flew above the edge. Sometimes they reached down and grabbed their skateboards as they soared through the air.

Lying on their tummies under the bushes, the Rabbids watched the skateboarders, fascinated.

Ding ding! Ding ding!

An ice-cream vendor pushed his cart along a sidewalk near the skateboarding bowl. As his cart

rolled along, bells rang, letting everyone know the ice-cream man had arrived.

"Break time!" yelled one of the skateboarders. He jumped off his board and ran toward the ice-cream guy. So did the other two skateboarders.

Which left three unattended skateboards by the big concrete bowl. . . .

CHAPTER 8:

RABBIDS ON BOARDS

Agent Glyker sat in his crummy car writing up notes from his encounter with the Rabbids at the baseball stadium.

AGENT GLYKER'S NOTES

- Rabbids seem to be attracted to public events with large crowds. Perhaps they want an audience for their message to Earth. Whatever that is.

- Rabbids have somehow managed to attract followers, like Courtney.

- When you throw trash at a Rabbid, it doesn't mind. It just picks up the trash and plays with it.

Glyker was considering erasing this last item, since it didn't seem all that useful, when his cell phone rang. He looked at the screen.

Director Stern.

Should he ignore the call? Let it go to voice mail? Or answer and get it over with?

He decided to get it over with. He pressed a button on the phone, and before he could finish saying, "Glyker, Secret Agent Second Class," his uncle was bellowing at him.

"GLYKER! JUST WHAT DO YOU THINK YOU'RE DOING OUT THERE? I THOUGHT I TOLD YOU TO CATCH A RABBID!" Stern shouted.

"You did, Uncle Jim—I mean, Director Stern," Glyker stammered.

"THEN WHY AM I GETTING REPORTS OF RABBIDS AT THE BASEBALL STADIUM? RABBIDS RIDING SHOPPING CARTS? RABBIDS IN THE SKATEBOARDING PARK?!"

"Skateboarding park?" Glyker answered, excited at this new piece of information. "I'm on my way!"

"BUT I'M NOT DONE YELLING AT—"

Glyker hung up, started his crummy old car (on the third try), and drove to the city's skateboarding park.

Glyker parked his car, jumped out, and ran toward the concrete bowl. Three young skate-boarders slouched up to him. "Are you the dude who's going to get our skateboards back from those stupid Rabbids?" they drawled.

Glyker squared his shoulders. "I sure am," he said. "Glyker, Secret Agent Second—"

"We're superupset," interrupted one of the skateboarders, looking not at all upset. In fact, he looked as though he were ready for a nap. "They took our boards, man!"

"Did you try to take them back?" Glyker asked.

The skateboarder looked puzzled. "You mean, do something? Like, violent? Not cool, bro."

"Whatever," said another skateboarder. "Just get our boards back. We're gonna go get something to eat. I'm starving."

He finished his ice-cream cone and walked away. The other two followed him, staring at their cell phones. One of them posted a Tweet about the Rabbids stealing his skateboard at the park, and some secret agent dude coming to help.

From the concrete bowl, Glyker could hear the Rabbids whooping and laughing. "BWOO! BWHEE! BWAAAH! HA HA!"

He didn't want to scare them off, so Glyker got down on his stomach and crawled through the grass toward the bowl.

When he reached the edge, he peered in.

The Rabbids were riding the skateboards around the inside of the concrete bowl, having a great time. One sat on his skateboard. Another lay on his back. The third lay on his stomach, pushing the ground with his hands. Occasionally they crashed right into each other, but they didn't seem to mind. It made them laugh even harder.

"BWAH HA HA HA HA!"

"This is terrible," Glyker thought to himself. "They're not wearing helmets! Or kneepads! Or elbow pads! Or anything!"

Slowly and carefully, Glyker pulled the Stopomizer out of his pocket. (He really wished he had some kind of a cool holster to carry it in. Maybe the kind that went under your armpit. Although that might be uncomfortable. The Stopomizer was kind of bulky.)

"Concentrate!" he thought. "Stop thinking about holsters!"

Just as he was deciding that the Rabbid lying on his back would make the best target, Glyker heard a familiar voice.

A horribly familiar voice.

"THERE YOU ARE, RABBIDS!" Courtney squealed. "I'M COMING!"

Courtney had seen the skateboarder's Tweet. She glided up to the edge of the bowl wearing in-line skates. She only hesitated for a moment, then dropped down into the bowl.

"WHEEE!" she yelled.

As they whipped around the bottom of the bowl, the Rabbids stared at Courtney. The red-headed creature from the place with the green field. They were getting tired of being bothered by her.

The leader barked a command to his two fellow invaders. "Bwah-bwah. Bwah!"

The three Rabbids jumped off their skate-boards and ran toward Courtney. She frowned. "I told you guys to stay away from that agent! And now he's some-where around here!"

Agent Glyker really wanted to use the Stopomizer on the Rabbids, but unfortunately, Courtney had skated right in between him and the invaders.

Two of the Rabbids grabbed Courtney's hands,
while the third one got behind her and pushed.

"Hey!" she said, surprised. "What are you doing?"

Running as fast as they could, the Rabbids took Courtney up a ramp and out of the concrete bowl. Then they kept on going. "Where are we going?" she asked nervously.

The Rabbids just kept on pulling and pushing Courtney, who seemed to finally realize that Rabbids weren't all that cute and cuddly after all.

"HELP!" Courtney screamed.

CHAPTER 9:
THEY'LL DRIVE YOU CRAZY

Courtney had no idea where the Rabbids were taking her.

But they didn't either. Their plan hadn't gone beyond "grab her and take her away somewhere so she'll stop bugging us."

So they just kept running through the park. And Courtney kept screaming.

"HALT!" Glyker yelled as he leaped onto the

sidewalk in front of them. He'd managed to cut straight across when the sidewalk took a big curve. So now he was blocking the Rabbids.

And he was pointing the Stopomizer right at them.

"Bwah?" said the leader, puzzled.

"I SAID HALT!" Glyker repeated as the Rabbids moved slowly forward.

BRZZZZT! Glyker fired the Stopomizer, planning to hit one of the Rabbids in front.

Unfortunately, it didn't work out that way.

Because just as Glyker pulled the Stopomizer's trigger, the Rabbids shoved Courtney forward, right at Glyker. The Stopomizer's ray hit Courtney, and she immediately froze like a statue. She wasn't cold or icy, she just completely stopped moving.

The Rabbids immediately let go of her and ran. As she fell toward the sidewalk, Glyker jumped forward and caught her.

When he looked up, the Rabbids were gone.

"Now what?" Glyker thought. "I can't just leave her here like this."

Luckily, though Courtney was completely stopped, the wheels on her skates weren't. They

still turned. Glyker found he could carefully push her ahead of him as he made his way along the sidewalk. He figured he'd roll her back to his car and then figure out what to do with her.

Except that when he reached the parking lot, his car wasn't there.

Still holding up Courtney, Glyker looked around wildly. Down the street, he saw his car, stopping and starting, weaving and zig-zagging.

There was a Rabbid at the wheel.

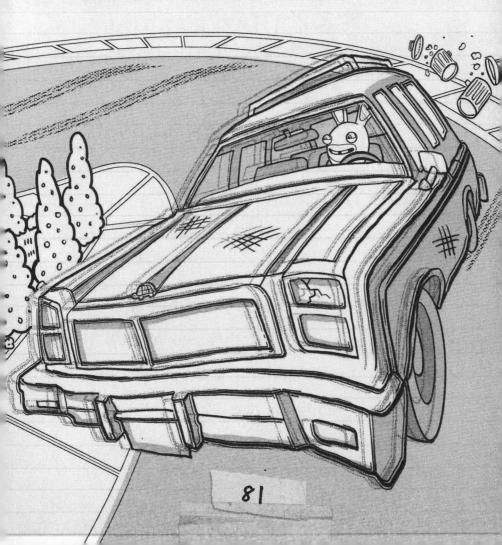

CHAPTER 10

STOP THAT RABBID!

Inside Glyker's car, one Rabbid was on the floor, pushing the pedals. He hit the brakes as often as he hit the gas, so the car kept stopping and starting.

The other two Rabbids were standing on the seat, turning the steering wheel. Each one of them wanted to steer. They kept jerking the wheel in different directions, so the car was swerving all over the road.

All three were yelling at each other. "BWAH!

BWAH BWAH BWAH BWAH BWAH!"

Glyker wanted to run after his car. But he couldn't leave Courtney. He had to grab her arms and keep rolling him behind her as he tried to catch up with the car.

Luckily for Glyker, the car stopped about as often as it went forward, so he was able to catch up with it in a couple of blocks.

"Pull over!" he yelled. "Stop the car! Get out! That's *my* car!"

The Rabbids had no idea what he was saying. They just stared at him.

They didn't notice the huge truck coming from the other direction.

HONK! HONK! The truck driver, Gus, was blasting his horn, warning the car to get out of the middle of the road. "Wait a minute," he said to himself, staring at the car. "Is that car being driven by . . . RABBIDS?!" *HONNNNNKKKK!*

At the last possible second, the car swerved over to the side of the road. It bumped over the curb and stopped.

Agent Glyker ran up to the car (still dragging Courtney) and yanked open the door. He aimed his Stopomizer right at the closest Rabbid.

The Rabbid put up his hands, looking scared.

Glyker hesitated just long enough for . . . a hand to reach around from behind him and grab the Stopomizer!

Courtney had come unstopped. "What are you DOING?!" she yelled at Glyker. She didn't seem to remember anything that had happened since Glyker had accidentally used the Stopomizer on her.

"Courtney, give me that!" Glyker said. "Right now!" He reached for the gadget. "My Stopomizer is not a toy. It's meant for trained professionals, like myself. . . ." Glyker puffed out his chest a little bit as he spoke.

But Courtney wasn't impressed. And neither were the Rabbids.

"Oh, you want this thing back?" she asked Glyker. "Well, too bad! I think it's time you learned what it's like to be chased around by a maniac with a Stopomizer or whatever you call it!"

Courtney ran around the car, reached in through the other door, and handed the Stopomizer to one of the Rabbids.

"Bwoooooh!" he said, delighted.

Horrified, Glyker carefully stretched his hand toward the Rabbid with the Stopomizer. "Come on, little guy," he coaxed gently. "Give it to me. Please."

The Rabbid looked at Glyker, confused. Then he looked at the Stopomizer. "Bwuh? Bwah?" he said.

"Hand it to me," Glyker said, reaching a little closer. Then . . .

BRZZZZZZT!

When Agent Glyker became unstopped, all he saw was Courtney. No Rabbids.

"Are you all right?" Courtney asked. "You were, like, completely stopped."

"I'm fine," Glyker said. "Where are the Rabbids?"

Courtney pointed up into the sky. "They're gone. A spaceship came. They got in it and left. And they took your whatchamacallit with them. I guess you were right about them. Sorry I didn't really listen to you before. "

Agent Glyker nodded, grateful for her apology, even if it did sound a little halfhearted. "Yeah, but they'll be back. You may still get to hug a Rabbid someday."

Courtney made a face. "Ew," she said. "Hug them? I don't think so. From now on, I'm only interested in . . ." She looked around, thinking. Then she spotted someone walking a big, fluffy dog. "Dogs! I love dogs!"

She ran off after a dog and his owner. "Hey, mister!" she called. "May I hug your dog? *Please?*"

Shaking his head, Agent Glyker walked over to see if his car would start. "Next time," he thought to himself. "I'll get those Rabbids next time for sure!"

93

Glyker's To-Do List:

1. Ask ~~Uncle Jim~~ Director Stern for demonstration to use gadgets in gadget closet

2. Get car fixed.

3. Find a new favorite baseball team.

4. Work on blueprints for top-secret infiltration project.

5. Update online dating profile.

large mouth

bent tongue